Reprint Publishing

FOR PEOPLE WHO GO FOR ORIGINALS.

www.reprintpublishing.com

" PST !"

A Proposal
Under Difficulties

A Farce

By
John Kendrick Bangs

Illustrated

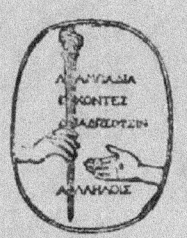

Harper & Brothers Publishers
New York and London
1905

CAST OF CHARACTERS

ROBERT YARDSLEY, } *suitors for the hand of*
JACK BARLOW, } *Miss Andrews.*
DOROTHY ANDREWS, *a much-loved young woman.*
JENNIE, *a housemaid.*
HICKS, *a coachman, who does not appear.*

A PROPOSAL UNDER DIFFICULTIES

The scene is laid in a fashionable New York drawing-room. The time is late in October, and Wednesday afternoon. The curtain rising shows an empty room. A bell rings. After a pause the front-door is heard opening and closing. Enter YARDSLEY *through portière at rear of room.*

Yardsley. Ah! So far so good; but I wish it were over. I've had the nerve to get as far as the house and into it, but how much further my courage will carry me I can't say. Confound it! Why is it, I wonder, that men get so rattled when they're head over heels in love, and want to ask the fair object of their af-

3

fections to wed? I can't see. Now I'm brave enough among men. I'm not afraid of anything that walks, except Dorothy Andrews, and generally I'm not afraid of her. Stopping runaway teams and talking back to impudent policemen have been my delight. I've even been courageous enough to submit a poem in person to the editor of a comic weekly, and yet here this afternoon I'm all of a tremble. And for what reason? Just because I've co-come to ask Dorothy Andrews to change her name to Mrs. Bob Yardsley; as if that were such an unlikely thing for her to do. Gad! I'm almost inclined to despise myself. (*Surveys himself in the mirror at one end of the room. Then walking up to it and peering intently at his reflection, he continues.*) Bah! you coward! Afraid of a woman—a sweet little woman like

4

A Proposal Under Difficulties

Dorothy. You ought to be ashamed of yourself, Bob Yardsley. *She* won't hurt you. Brace up and propose like a man—like a real lover who'd go through fire for her sake, and all that. Ha! That's easy enough to talk about, but how shall I put it? That's the question. Let me see. How *do* men do it? I ought to buy a few good novels and select the sort of proposal I like; but not having a novel at hand, I must invent my own. How will it be? Something like this, I fancy. (*The portières are parted, and* JENNIE, *the maid, enters.* YARDSLEY *does not observe her entrance.*) I'll get down on my knees. A man on his knees is a pitiable object, and pity, they say, is akin to love. Maybe she'll pity me, and after that—well, perhaps pity's cousin will arrive. (*The maid advances, but* YARDSLEY *is so intent upon*

A Proposal Under Difficulties

his proposal that he still fails to observe her. She stands back of the sofa, while he, gazing downward, kneels before it.) I'll say: "Divine creature! At last we are alone, and I — ah — I can speak

"'DIVINE CREATURE'"

freely the words that have been in my heart to say to you for so long—oh, so long a time." (JENNIE *appears sur-*

prised.) "I have never even hinted at how I feel towards you. I have concealed my love, fearing lest by too sudden a betrayal of my feelings I should lose all." (*Aside.*) Now for a little allusion to the poets. Poetry, they say, is a great thing for proposals. "You know, dearest, you must know, how the poet has phrased it — 'Fain would I fall but that I fear to climb.' But now—now I must speak. An opportunity like this may not occur again. Will you — will you be my wife?"

> [JENNIE *gives a little scream of delight.*

Jennie. Oh, Mr. Yardsley, this is so suddent like and unexpected, and me so far beneath you!

> [YARDSLEY *looks up and is covered with confusion.*

7

Yardsley. Great Scott! What have I done?

Jennie. But of course it ain't for the likes of me to say no to—

Yardsley (rising). For Heaven's sake, Jennie—do be sensi— Don't—say— Jennie, why—ah— (*Aside.*) Oh, confound it! What the deuce shall I say? What's the matter with my tongue? Where's my vocabulary? A word! a word! my kingdom for a word! (*Aloud.*) Now, Jen—

Jennie (coyly). I has been engaged to Mr. Hicks, the coach gentleman, sir, but—

Yardsley. Good! good! I congratulate you, Jennie. Hicks is a very fine fellow. Drives like a — like a driver, Jennie, a born driver. I've seen him many a time sitting like a king on his box—yes, indeed. Noticed him often. Admired him. Gad, Jennie, I'll see

8

him myself and tell him; and what is more, Jennie, I'll—I'll give Hicks a fine present.

Jennie. Yes, sir; I has no doubt as how you'll be doin' the square thing by Hicks, for, as I was a-sayin', I has been engaged like to him, an' he has some rights; but I think as how, if I puts it to him right like, and tells him what a nice gentleman you are (*a ring is heard at the front-door*), it 'll be all right, sir. But there goes the bell and I must run, Mr. Yardsley. (*Ecstatically kissing her hand.*) Bob!

Yardsley (*with a convulsive gasp*). Bob? Jennie! You—er—you misun— (JENNIE, *with a smile of joy and an ecstatic glance at* YARDSLEY, *dances from the room to attend the door.* YARDSLEY *throws himself into a chair.*) Well, I'll be teetotally— Awh! It's too dead easy proposing to somebody you don't know you are proposing to. What a kettle of fish this is, to be sure! Oh, pshaw! that woman can't be serious. She must know I didn't mean it for her. But if she doesn't, good Lord! what becomes of me? (*Rises, and paces up and down the room nervously. After a moment he pauses before the glass.*) I ought to be considerably dishevelled by this. I feel as if I'd been drawn through a knot-hole — or — or dropped into a stone-crusher—that's it, a stone-crusher — a ten-million horse-power stone-crusher. Let's see how you look, you poor idiot.

> [*As he is stroking his hair and re-arranging his tie he talks in pantomime at himself in the glass. In a moment* JENNIE *ushers* MR. JACK BARLOW *into the room.*

10

A Proposal Under Difficulties

Jennie. Miss Andrews will be down in a minute, sir.

> [BARLOW *takes arm-chair and sits gazing ahead of him. Neither he nor* YARDSLEY *perceives the other.* JENNIE *tiptoes to one side, and, tossing a kiss at* YARDSLEY, *retires.*

Barlow. Now for it. I shall leave this house to-day the happiest or the most miserable man in creation, and I rather think the odds are in my favor. Why shouldn't they be? Egad! I can very well understand how a woman could admire me. I admire myself, rather. I confess candidly that I do not consider myself half bad, and Dorothy has always seemed to feel that way herself. In fact, the other night in the Perkinses' conservatory she seemed to be quite ready for a proposal. I'd have done it then and there if it hadn't been for that confounded Bob Yardsley—

Yardsley (*turning sharply about*). Eh? Somebody spoke my name. A man, too. Great Heavens! I hope Jennie's friend Hicks isn't here. I don't want to have a scene with Hicks. (*Discovering* BARLOW.) Oh—ah—why—hullo, Barlow! You here?

Barlow (*impatiently, aside*). Hang it! Yardsley's here too! The man's always turning up when he's not wanted. (*Aloud.*) Ah! why, Bob, how are you? What 're you doing here?

Yardsley. What do you suppose— tuning the piano? I'm here because I want to be. And you?

Barlow. For the same reason that you are.

Yardsley (*aside*). Gad! I hope not.

12

A Proposal Under Difficulties

(*Aloud.*) Indeed? The great mind act again? Run in the same channel, and all that? Glad to see you. (*Aside.*) May the saints forgive me that fib! But this fellow must be got rid of.

Barlow (*embarrassed*). So'm I. Always glad to see myself—I mean you—anywhere. Won't you sit down?

Yardsley. Thanks. Very kind of you, I'm sure. (*Aside.*) He seems very much at home. Won't I sit down?—as if he'd inherited the chairs! Humph! I'll show him.

Barlow. What say?

Yardsley. I—ah—oh, I was merely remarking that I thought it was rather pleasant out to-day.

Barlow. Yes, almost too fine to be shut up in-doors. Why aren't you driving, or — or playing golf, or — ah — or being out-doors somewhere? You need exercise, old man, you look a little pale. (*Aside.*) I must get him away from here somehow. Deuced awkward having another fellow about when you mean to propose to a woman.

Yardsley. Oh, I'm well enough!

Barlow (*solicitously*). You don't look it—by Jove, you don't. (*Suddenly inspired.*) No, you don't, Bob. You overestimate your strength. It's very wrong to overestimate one's strength. People —ah—people have died of it. Why, I'll bet you a hat you can't start now and walk up to Central Park and back in an hour. Come. I'll time you. (*Rises and takes out watch.*) It is now four-ten. I'll wager you can't get back here before five-thirty. Eh? Let me get your hat.

[*Starts for door.*

Yardsley (*with a laugh*). Oh no; I

don't bet — after four. But I say, did you see Billie Wilkins?

Barlow (returning in despair). Nope.

Yardsley (aside). Now for a bit of strategy. (*Aloud.*) He was look-ing for you at the club. (*Aside.*) Splen-did lie! (*Aloud.*) Had seats for the — ah — the Metropolitan to-night. Said he was look-ing for you.

"I'LL TIME YOU"

Wants you to go with him. (*Aside.*) That ought to start him along.

Barlow. I'll go with him.

Yardsley (eagerly). Well, you'd better let him know at once, then. Better run around there and catch him while there's time. He said if he didn't see you before half-past four he'd get Tom Parker to go. Fine show to - night. Wouldn't lose the opportunity if I were you. (*Looking at his watch.*) You'll just about have time to do it now if you start at once.

    [*Grasps* BARLOW *by arm, and tries to force him out.* BARLOW *holds back, and is about to remonstrate, when* DOROTHY *enters. Both men rush to greet her;* YARDSLEY *catches her left hand,* BARLOW *her right.*

Dorothy (*slightly embarrassed*). Why, how do you do—this is an unexpected pleasure — both of you? Excuse my left hand, Mr. Yardsley; I should have given you the other if—if you'd given me time.

A Proposal Under Difficulties

Yardsley. Don't mention it, I pray. The unexpectedness is wholly mine, Miss Andrews — I mean — ah — the pleasure is—

Barlow. Wholly mine.

Dorothy (withdrawing her hands from both and sitting down). I haven't seen either of you since the Perkinses' dance.

"START AT ONCE"

Wasn't it a charming affair?

Yardsley. Delightful I — ah — I didn't know that the Perkinses—

Barlow (interrupting). It was a good deal of a crush, though. As Mrs. Van Darling said to me, "You always meet—"

A Proposal Under Difficulties

Yardsley. It's a pity Perkins isn't more of a society man, though, don't you think?

Dorothy. Oh, I don't know. I've always found him very pleasant. He is so sincere.

Barlow. Isn't he, though? He looked bored to death all through the dance.

Yardsley. I thought so too. I was watching him while you were talking to him, Barlow, and such a look of ennui I never saw on a man's face.

Barlow. Humph!

Dorothy. Are you going to Mrs. Van Darling's dinner?

Barlow. Yes; I received my bid last night. You?

Dorothy. Oh yes!

Yardsley (gloomily). I can't go very well. I'm—ah—engaged for Tuesday.

Barlow. Well, I hope you've let Mrs.

18

Van Darling know. She's a stickler for promptness in accepting or declining her invitations. If you haven't, I'll tell her for you. I'm to see her to-night.

Yardsley. Oh no! Never mind. I'll —I'll attend to it.

Barlow. Oh, of course. But it's just as well she should know in advance. You might forget it, you know. I'll tell her; it's no trouble to me.

Dorothy. Of course not, and she can get some one to take your place.

Yardsley (desperately). Oh, don't say anything about it. Fact is, she—ah— she hasn't invited me.

Barlow. Ah! (*Aside.*) I knew that all along. Oh, but I'm clever!

Dorothy (hastily, to relieve YARDSLEY'S *embarrassment).* Have you seen Irving, Mr. Yardsley?

Yardsley. Yes.

Barlow (*suspiciously*). What in? I haven't seen you at any of the first nights.

Yardsley (*with a grin*). In the grill-room at the Players'.

Barlow (*aside*). Bah!

Dorothy (*laughing*). You are so bright, Mr. Yardsley.

Barlow (*forcing a laugh*). Ha, ha, ha! Why, yes—very clever that. It ought to have a Gibson picture over it, that joke. It would help it. Those Gibson pictures are fine, I think. Carry any kind of joke, eh?

Yardsley. Yes, they frequently do.

Dorothy. I'm so glad you both like Gibson, for I just dote on him. I have one of his originals in my portfolio. I'll get it if you'd like to see it.

    [*She rises and goes to the corner of the room, where there stands a portfolio-case.*

A Proposal Under Difficulties

Yardsley (aside). What a bore Barlow is! Hang him! I must get rid of him somehow.

[BARLOW *meanwhile is assisting* DOROTHY.

Yardsley (looking around at the others). Jove! he's off in the corner with her. Can't allow that, for the fact is Barlow's just a bit dangerous—to me.

Dorothy (rummaging through portfolio). Why, it *was* here—

Barlow. Maybe it's in this other portfolio.

Yardsley (joining them). Yes, maybe it is. That's a good idea. If it isn't in one portfolio maybe it's in another. Clever thought! I may be bright, Miss Andrews, but you must have observed that Barlow is thoughtful.

Dorothy (with a glance at BARLOW*).* Yes, Mr. Yardsley, I have noticed the latter.

A Proposal Under Difficulties

Barlow. Tee-hee! that's one on you, Bob.

Yardsley (obtuse). Ha, ha! Yes. Why, of course! Ha, ha, ha! For repartee I have always said — polite repartee, of course—Miss Andrews is— (*Aside.*) Now what the dickens did she mean by that?

Dorothy. I can't find it here. Let— me think. Where—can—it—be?

Barlow (striking thoughtful attitude). Yes, where can it be? Let me do your thinking for you, Miss Dorothy. (*Then softly to her.*) Always!

Yardsley (mocking BARLOW). Yes! Let *me* think! (*Points his finger at his forehead and assumes tragic attitude. Then stalks to the front of stage in manner of burlesque Hamlet.*) Come, thought, come. Shed the glory of thy greatness full on me, and thus confound mine enemies. Where the deuce is that Gibson?

Dorothy. Oh, I remember. It's upstairs. I took it up with me last night. I'll ring for Jennie, and have her get it.

Yardsley (aside, and in consternation). Jennie! Oh, thunder! I'd forgotten her. I do hope she remembers not to forget herself.

Barlow. What say?

Yardsley. Nothing; only—ah—only that I thought it was very—very pleasant out.

Barlow. That's what you said before.

Yardsley (indignantly). Well, what of it? It's the truth. If you don't believe it, go outside and see for yourself.

[JENNIE *appears at the door in response to* DOROTHY'S *ring. She*

23

glances demurely at YARDSLEY,
who tries to ignore her presence.

Dorothy. Jennie, go up to my room and look on the table in the corner, and bring me down the portfolio you will find there. The large brown one that belongs in the stand over there.

Jennie (*dazed*). Yessum. And shall I be bringin' lemons with it?

Dorothy. Lemons, Jennie?

Jennie. You always does have lemons with your tea, mum.

Dorothy. I didn't mention tea. I want you to get my portfolio from upstairs. It is on the table in the corner of my room.

[*Looks at* JENNIE *in surprise.*

Jennie. Oh, excuse me, mum. I didn't hear straight.

[*She casts a languishing glance at* YARDSLEY *and disappears.*

24

A Proposal Under Difficulties

Yardsley (noting the glance, presumably aside). Confound that Jennie!

Barlow (overhearing YARDSLEY). What's that? Confound that Jennie? Why say confound that Jennie? Why do you wish Jennie to be confounded?

Yardsley (nervously). I didn't say that. I—ah—I merely said that—that Jennie appeared to be—ah—confounded.

Dorothy. She certainly is confused. I cannot understand it at all. Ordinarily I have rather envied Jennie her composure.

Yardsley. Oh, I suppose — it's — it's —it's natural for a young girl—a servant—sometimes to lose her—equipoise, as it were, on occasions. If we lose ours at times, why not Jennie? Eh? Huh?

Barlow. Certainly.

Yardsley. Of course — ha — trained

servants are hard to get these days, anyhow. Educated people — ah — go into other professions, such as law, and —ah—the ministry—and—

Dorothy. Well, never mind. Let's talk of something more interesting than Jennie. Going to the Chrysanthemum Show, Mr. Barlow?

Barlow. I am; wouldn't miss it for the world. Do you know, really now, the chrysanthemum, in my opinion, is the most human-looking flower we have. The rose is too beautiful, too perfect, for me. The chrysanthemum, on the other hand—

Yardsley (interrupting). Looks so like a football-player's head it appeals to your sympathies? Well, perhaps you are right. I never thought of it in that light before, but—

Dorothy (smiling). Nor I; but now

that you mention it, it does look that way, doesn't it?

Barlow (*not wishing to disagree with* DOROTHY). Very much. Droll idea, though. Just like Bob, eh? Very, very droll. Bob's always dro—

Yardsley (*interrupting*). When I see a man walking down the avenue with a chrysanthemum in his button-hole, I always think of a wild Indian wearing a scalp for decorative purposes.

> [BARLOW *and* DOROTHY *laugh at this, and during their mirth* JENNIE *enters with the portfolio. She hands it to* DOROTHY. DOROTHY *rests it on the arm of her chair, and,* BARLOW *looking over one shoulder, she goes through it.* JENNIE *in passing out throws another kiss to* YARDSLEY.

Yardsley (under his breath, stamping his foot). Awgh!

Barlow. What say?

[DOROTHY *looks up, surprised.*

Yardsley. I—I didn't say anything. My—ah—my shoe had a piece of—ah—

Barlow. Oh, say lint, and be done with it.

Yardsley (relieved, and thankful for the suggestion). Why, how did you know? It did, you know. Had a piece of lint on it, and I tried to get it off by stamping, that's all.

Dorothy. Ah, here it is.

Yardsley. What? The lint?

Barlow. Ho! Is the world nothing but lint to you? Of course not—the Gibson. Charming, isn't it, Miss Dorothy?

Dorothy (holding the picture up). Fine. Just look at that girl. Isn't she pretty?

A Proposal Under Difficulties

Barlow. Very.

Dorothy. And such style, too.

Yardsley (looking over DOROTHY'S *other*

"CHARMING, ISN'T IT?"

shoulder). Yes, very pretty, and lots of style. (*Softly.*) Very—like some one —some one I know.

Barlow (overhearing). I think so myself, Yardsley. It's exactly like Josie Wilkins. By-the-way — ah — how is that little affair coming along, Bob?

Dorothy (*interested*). What! You don't mean to say— Why, *Mister* Yardsley!

Yardsley (*with a venomous glance at* BARLOW). Nonsense. Nothing in it. Mere invention of Barlow's. He's a regular Edison in his own way.

[DOROTHY *looks inquiringly at* BAR-
LOW.

Barlow (*to* YARDSLEY). Oh, don't be so sly about it, old fellow! *Every*body knows.

Yardsley. But I tell you there's nothing in it. I—I have different ideas entirely, and you—you know it — or, if you don't, you will shortly.

Dorothy. Oh! Then it's some one else, Mr. Yardsley? Well, now I *am* interested. Let's have a little confidential talk together. Tell *us*, Mr. Yardsley, tell Mr. Barlow and me, and maybe—I can't say for certain, of course —but maybe we can help you.

Barlow (gleefully rubbing his hands). Yes, old man; certainly. Maybe we —*we* can help you.

Yardsley (desperately). You can help me, both of you—but—but I can't very well tell you how.

Barlow. I'm willing to do all I can for you, my dear Bob. If you will only tell us her name I'll even go so far as to call, in your behalf, and propose for you.

Yardsley. Oh, thanks. You are very kind.

Dorothy. I think so too, Mr. Barlow. You are almost too kind, it seems to me.

Yardsley. Oh no; not too kind, Miss

Andrews. Barlow simply realizes that one who has proposed marriage to young girls as frequently as he has knows how the thing is done, and he wishes to give me the benefit of his experience. (*Aside.*) That's a facer for Barlow.

Barlow. Ha, ha, ha! Another joke, I suppose. You see, my dear Bob, that I am duly appreciative. I laugh. Ha, ha, ha! But I must say I laugh with some uncertainty. I don't know whether you intended that for a joke or for a staggerer. You should provide your conversation with a series of printed instructions for the listener. Get a lot of cards, and have printed on one, "Please laugh"; on another, "Please stagger"; on another, "Kindly appear confused." Then when you mean to be jocose hand over the laughter card, and so on. Shall I stagger?

A Proposal Under Difficulties

Dorothy. I think that Mr. Yardsley meant that for a joke. Didn't you, Mr. Yardsley?

Yardsley. Why, certainly. Of course. I don't really believe Barlow ever had sand enough to propose to any one. Did you, Jack?

Barlow (indignant). Well, I rather think I have.

Dorothy. Ho, ho! Then you *are* an experienced proposer, Mr. Barlow?

Barlow (confused). Why — er — well — um — I didn't exactly mean that, you know. I meant that—ah— if it ever came to the—er—the test, I think I could—I'd have sand enough, as Yardsley puts it, to do the thing properly, and without making a—ah—a Yardsley of myself.

Yardsley (bristling up). Now what do you mean by that?

A Proposal Under Difficulties

Dorothy. I think you are both of you horrid this afternoon. You are so quarrelsome. Do you two always quarrel, or is this merely a little afternoon's diversion got up for my especial benefit?

Barlow (*with dignity*). I never quarrel.

Yardsley. Nor I. I simply differ sometimes, that's all. I never had an unpleasant word with Jack in my life. Did I, Jack?

Barlow. Never. I always avoid a fracas, however great the provocation.

Dorothy (*desperately*). Then let us have a cup of tea together and be more sociable. I have always noticed that tea promotes sociability—haven't you, Mr. Yardsley?

Yardsley. Always. (*Aside.*) Among women.

Barlow. What say?

A Proposal Under Difficulties

[DOROTHY *rises and rings the bell for*
    JENNIE.

Yardsley. I say that I am very fond
of tea.

Barlow. So am I—here.

[*Rises and looks at pictures.* YARDS-
    LEY *meanwhile sits in moody silence.*

Dorothy (returning). You seem to
have something on your mind, Mr.
Yardsley. I never knew you to be so
solemn before.

Yardsley. I have something on my
mind, Miss Dorothy. It's—

Barlow (coming forward). Wise man,
cold weather like this. It would be
terrible if you let your mind go out in
cold weather without anything on it.
Might catch cold in your idea.

Dorothy. I wonder why Jennie doesn't
come? I shall have to ring again.

[*Pushes electric button again.*

35

A Proposal Under Difficulties

Yardsley (with an effort at brilliance).
The kitchen belle doesn't seem to
work.

Dorothy. Ordinarily she does, but
she seems to be upset by something this
afternoon. I'm afraid she's in love.
If you will excuse me a moment I will
go and prepare the tea myself.

Barlow. Do; good! Then we shall
not need the sugar.

Yardsley. You might omit the spoons
too, after a remark like that, Miss
Dorothy.

Dorothy. We'll omit Mr. Barlow's
spoon. I'll bring some for you and me.

[*She goes out.*

Yardsley (with a laugh). That's one
on you, Barlow. But I say, old man
(*taking out his watch and snapping the
cover to three or four times*), it's getting
very late—after five now. If you want

36

to go with Billie Wilkins you'd better take up your hat and walk. I'll say good-bye to Miss Andrews for you.

Barlow. Thanks. Too late now. You said Billie wouldn't wait after four-thirty.

Yardsley. Did I say four-thirty? I meant five-thirty. Anyhow, Billie isn't over-prompt. Better go.

Barlow. You seem mighty anxious to get rid of me.

Yardsley. I? Not at all, my dear boy—not at all. I'm very, very fond of you, but I thought you'd prefer opera to me. Don't you see? That's where my modesty comes in. You're so fond of a good chat I thought you'd want to go to-night. Wilkins has a box.

Barlow. You said seats a little while ago.

Yardsley. Of course I did. And why

37

not? There are seats in boxes. Didn't you know that?

Barlow. Look here, Yardsley, what's up, anyhow? You've been deuced queer to-day. What are you after?

"WHAT'S UP, ANYHOW?"

Yardsley (tragically). Shall I confide in you? Can I, with a sense of confidence that you will not betray me?

38

A Proposal Under Difficulties

Barlow (eagerly). Yes, Bob. Go on. What is it? I'll never give you away, and I *may* be able to give you some good advice.

Yardsley. I am here to—to—to rob the house! Business has been bad, and one must live.

[BARLOW *looks at him in disgust.*

Yardsley (mockingly). You have my secret, John Barlow. Remember that it was wrung from me in confidence. You must not betray me. Turn your back while I surreptitiously remove the piano and the gas-fixtures, won't you?

Barlow (looking at him thoughtfully). Yardsley, I have done you an injustice.

Yardsley. Indeed?

Barlow. Yes. Some one claimed, at the club, the other day, that you were the biggest donkey in existence, and I denied it. I was wrong, old man, I was wrong, and I apologize. You are.

Yardsley. You are too modest, Jack. You forget—yourself.

Barlow. Well, perhaps I do; but I've nothing to conceal, and you have. You've been behaving in a most incomprehensible fashion this afternoon, as if you owned the house.

Yardsley. Well, what of it? Do you own it?

Barlow. No, I don't, but—

Yardsley. But you hope to. Well, I have no such mercenary motive. I'm not after the house.

Barlow (*bristling up*). After the house? Mercenary motive? I demand an explanation of those words. What do you mean?

Yardsley. I mean this, Jack Barlow: I mean that I am here for—for my own

40

reasons; but you—you have come here for the purpose of—

[DOROTHY *enters with a tray, upon which are the tea things.*

Barlow (*about to retort to* YARDSLEY, *perceiving* DOROTHY). Ah! Let me assist you.

Dorothy. Thank you so much. I really believe I never needed help more. (*She delivers the tray to* BARLOW, *who sets it on the table.* DOROTHY, *exhausted, drops into a chair.*) Fan me—quick—or I shall faint. I've — I've had an awful time, and I really don't know what to do!

Barlow and *Yardsley* (*together*). Why, what's the matter?

Yardsley. I hope the house isn't on fire?

Barlow. Or that you haven't been robbed?

A Proposal Under Difficulties

Dorothy. No, no; nothing like that. It's—it's about Jennie.

Yardsley (nervously). Jennie? Wha —wha—what's the matter with Jennie?

Dorothy. I only wish I knew. I—

Yardsley (aside). I'm glad you don't.

Barlow. What say?

Yardsley. I didn't say anything. Why should I say anything? I haven't anything to say. If people who had nothing to say would not insist upon talking, you'd be—

Dorothy. I heard the poor girl weeping down - stairs, and when I went to the dumb-waiter to ask her what was the matter, I heard—I heard a man's voice.

Yardsley. Man's voice?

Barlow. Man's voice is what Miss Andrews said.

Dorothy. Yes; it was Hicks, our

coachman, and he was dreadfully angry about something.

Yardsley (sinking into chair). Good Lord! Hicks! Angry! At — something!

Dorothy. He was threatening to kill somebody.

Yardsley. This grows worse and worse! Threatening to kill somebody! D-did-did you o-over-overhear huh-huh-whom he was going to kuk-kill?

Barlow. What's the matter with you, Yardsley? Are you going to die of fright, or have you suddenly caught a chill?

Dorothy. Oh, I hope not! Don't die here, anyhow, Mr. Yardsley. If you must die, please go home and die. I couldn't stand another shock to-day. Why, really, I was nearly frightened to death. I don't know now but what

A Proposal Under Difficulties

I ought to send for the police, Hicks was so violent.

Barlow. Perhaps she and Hicks have had a lovers' quarrel.

Yardsley. Very likely; very likely, indeed. I think that is no doubt the explanation of the whole trouble. Lovers will quarrel. They were engaged, you know.

Dorothy (surprised). No, I didn't know it. Were they? Who told you?

Yardsley (discovering his mistake). Why — er — wasn't it you said so, Miss Dorothy? Or you, Barlow?

Barlow. I have not the honor of the young woman's confidence, and so could not have given you the information.

Dorothy. I didn't know it, so how could I have told you?

Yardsley (desperately). Then I must

have dreamed it. I do have the queerest dreams sometimes, but there's nothing strange about this one, anyhow. Parlor-maids frequently do — er — become engaged to coachmen and butlers and that sort of thing. It isn't a rare occurrence at all. If I'd said she was engaged to Billie Wilkins, or to—to Barlow here—

Barlow. Or to yourself.

Yardsley. Sir? What do you mean to insinuate? That I am engaged to Jennie?

Barlow. I never said so.

Dorothy. Oh, dear, let us have the tea. You quarrelsome men are just wearing me out. Mr. Barlow, do you want cream in yours?

Barlow. If you please ; and one lump of sugar. (DOROTHY *pours it out.*) Thanks.

A Proposal Under Difficulties

Dorothy. Mr. Yardsley?

Yardsley. Just a little, Miss Andrews. No cream, and no sugar.

[DOROTHY *prepares a cup for* YARDSLEY. *He is about to take it when—*

Dorothy. Well, I declare! *It's nothing but hot water! I forgot the tea entirely!*

Barlow (with a laugh). Oh, never mind. Hot water is good for dyspepsia.

[*With a significant look at* YARDSLEY.

Yardsley. It depends on how you get it, Mr. Barlow. I've known men who've got dyspepsia from living in hot water too much.

[*As* YARDSLEY *speaks the portière is violently clutched from without, and* JENNIE'S *head is thrust into the room. No one observes her.*

Barlow. Well, my cup is very satisfactory to me, Miss Dorothy. Fact is, I've always been fond of cambric tea, and this is just right.

Yardsley (patronizingly). It *is* good for children.

Jennie (trying to attract YARDSLEY'S *attention).* Pst!

Yardsley. My mamma lets me have it Sunday nights.

Dorothy. Ha, ha, ha!

Barlow. Another joke? Good. Let me enjoy it, too. Hee, hee!

Jennie. Pst!

[BARLOW *looks around;* JENNIE *hastily withdraws her head.*

Barlow. I didn't know you had steam heat in this house.

Dorothy. We haven't. What put such an idea as that into your head?

Barlow. Why, I thought I heard the hissing of steam, the click of a radiator,

47

or something of that sort back by the door.

Yardsley. Maybe the house is haunted.

Dorothy. I fancy it was your imagination; or perhaps it was the wind blowing through the hall. The pantry window is open.

Barlow. I guess maybe that's it. How fine it must be in the country now!

[JENNIE *pokes her head in through the portières again, and follows it with her arm and hand, in which is a feather-duster, which she waves wildly in an endeavor to attract* YARDSLEY'S *attention.*

Dorothy. Divine. I should so love to be out of town still. It seems to me people always make a great mistake returning to the city so early in the fall.

48

A Proposal Under Difficulties

The country is really at its best at this time of year.

> [YARDSLEY *turns half around, and is about to speak, when he catches sight of the now almost hysterical* JENNIE *and her feather-duster.*

Barlow. Yes; I think so too. I was at Lenox last week, and the foliage was gorgeous.

Yardsley (*feeling that he must say something*). Yes. I suppose all the feathers on the maple - trees are turning red by this time.

Dorothy. Feathers, Mr. Yardsley?

Barlow. Feathers?

Yardsley (*with a furtive glance at* JENNIE). Ha, ha! What an absurd slip! Did I say feathers? I meant—I meant leaves, of course. All the leaves on the dusters are turning.

Barlow. I don't believe you know

what you do mean. Who ever heard of leaves on dusters? What are dusters? Do you know, Miss Dorothy?

> [*As he turns to* Miss Andrews, Yardsley *tries to wave* Jennie *away. She beckons with her arms more wildly than ever, and* Yardsley *silently speaks the words,* "Go away."

Dorothy. I'm sure I don't know of any tree by that name, but then I'm not a—not a what?

Yardsley (with a forced laugh). Tree-ologist.

Dorothy. What are dusters, Mr. Yardsley?

Barlow. Yes, old man, tell us. I'm anxious to find out myself.

Yardsley (aside). So am I. What the deuce are dusters, for this occasion only? (*Aloud.*) What? Never heard of dust-

A Proposal Under Difficulties

ers? Ho! Why, dear me, where have you been all your lives? (*Aside.*) Must gain time to think up what dusters are. (*Aloud.*) Why, they're as old as the hills.

Barlow. That may be, but I can't say I think your description is at all definite.

Dorothy. Do they look like maples?

Yardsley (*with an angry wave of his arms towards* JENNIE). Something—in fact, very much. They're exactly like them. You can hardly tell them from oaks.

Barlow. Oaks?

Yardsley. I said oaks. Oaks! O-A-K-S!

Barlow. But oaks aren't like maples.

Yardsley. Well, who said they were? We were talking about oaks—and—er—

51

A Proposal Under Difficulties

and dusters. We—er—we used to have a row of them in front of our old house at— (*Aside.*) Now where the deuce did we have the old house? Never had one, but we must for the sake of the present situation. (*Aloud.*) Up at—at—Bryn-Mawr—or at—Troy, or some such place, and—at—they kept the—the dust of the highway from getting into the house. (*With a sigh of relief.*) And so, you see, they were called dusters. Thought every one knew that.

> As YARDSLEY *finishes*, JENNIE *loses*
> *her balance and falls headlong*
> *into the room.*

Dorothy (*starting up hastily*). Why, Jennie!

Yardsley (*staggering into chair*). That settles it. It's all up with me.

> [JENNIE *sobs, and, rising, rushes to*
> YARDSLEY'S *side.*

A Proposal Under Difficulties

Jennie. Save yourself; he's going to kill you!

Dorothy. Jennie! What is the meaning of this? Mr. Yardsley—can—can you shed any light on this mystery?

Yardsley (pulling himself together with a great effort). I? I assure you I can't, Miss Andrews. How could I? All I know is that somebody is —is going to kill me, though for what I haven't the slightest idea.

"WHY, JENNIE!"

Jennie (indignantly). Eh? What! Why, Mr. Yardsley—Bob!

Barlow. Bob?

Dorothy. Jennie! Bob?

Yardsley. Don't you call me Bob.

Jennie. It's Hicks.

[*Bursts out crying.*

Barlow. Hicks?

Dorothy. Jennie, Hicks isn't Bob. His name is George.

Yardsley (in a despairing rage). Hicks be—

Dorothy. Mr. Yardsley!

Yardsley (pulling himself together again). Bobbed. Hicks be Bobbed. That's what I was going to say.

Dorothy. What on earth does this all mean? I must have an explanation, Jennie. What have you to say for yourself?

Jennie. Why, I—

Yardsley. I tell you it isn't true. She's made it up out of whole cloth.

Barlow. What isn't true? She hasn't said anything yet.

54

A Proposal Under Difficulties

Yardsley (desperately). I refer to
what she's going to say. I'm a—a—
I'm a mind-reader, and I see it all as
plain as day.

Dorothy. I can best judge of the
truth of Jennie's words when she has
spoken them, Mr. Yardsley. Jennie,
you may explain, if you can. What
do you mean by Hicks killing Mr.
Yardsley, and why do you presume
to call Mr. Yardsley by his first
name?

Yardsley (aside). Heigho! My goose
is cooked.

Barlow. I fancy you wish you had
taken that walk I suggested now.

Yardsley. You always were a good
deal of a fancier.

Jennie. I hardly knows how to begin,
Miss Dorothy. I—I'm so flabbergasted
by all that's happened this afternoon,

mum, that I can't get my thoughts straight, mum.

Dorothy. Never mind getting your thoughts straight, Jennie. I do not want fiction. I want the truth.

Jennie. Well, mum, when a fine gentleman like Mr. Yardsley asks—

Yardsley. I tell you it isn't so.

Jennie. Indeed he did, mum.

Dorothy (impatiently). Did what?

Jennie. Axed me to marry him, mum.

Dorothy. Mr. Yardsley — asked — you—to—to marry him?

[BARLOW *whistles.*

Jennie (bursting into tears again). Yes, mum, he did, mum, right here in this room. He got down on his knees to me on that Proossian rug before the sofa, mum. I was standin' behind the sofa, havin' just come in to tell him

56

as how you'd be down shortly. He was
standin' before the lookin'-glass lookin'
at himself, an' when I come in he turns
around and goes down on his knees
and says such an importunity may not
occur again, mum; I've loved you very
long; and then he recited some pottery,
mum, and said would I be his wife.

Yardsley (*desperately*). Let me explain.

Dorothy. Wait, Mr. Yardsley; your
turn will come in a moment.

Barlow. Yes, it 'll be here, my boy;
don't fret about that. Take all the
time you need to make it a good one.
Gad! if this doesn't strain your imagination, nothing will.

Dorothy. Go on, Jennie. Then what
happened?

Yardsley (*with an injured expression*).
Do you expect me to stand here, Miss

Andrews, and hear this girl's horrible story?

Barlow. Then you know the story, do you, Yardsley? It's horrible, and you are innocent. My! you are a mind-reader with a vengeance.

Dorothy. Don't mind what these gentlemen say, Jennie, but go on.

[YARDSLEY *sinks into the arm-chair.* BARLOW *chuckles;* MISS ANDREWS *glances indignantly at him.*

Dorothy. Pardon me, Mr. Barlow. If there is any humor in the situation, I fail to see it.

Barlow (*seeing his error*). Nor, indeed, do I. I was not—ah—laughing from mirth. That chuckle was hysterics, Miss Dorothy, I assure you. There are some laughs that can hardly be differentiated from sobs.

Jennie. I was all took in a heap,

58

mum, to think of a fine gentleman like Mr. Yardsley proposing to me, mum, and I says the same. Says I, "Oh, Mr. Yardsley, this is so suddent like," whereat he looks up with a countenance so full o' pain that I hadn't the heart to refuse him; so, fergettin' Hicks for the moment, I says, kind o' soft like, certingly, sir. It ain't for the likes o' me to say no to the likes o' him.

Yardsley. Then you said you were engaged to Hicks. You know you did, Jennie.

Barlow. Ah! Then you admit the proposal?

Yardsley. Oh, Lord! Worse and worse! I—

Dorothy. Jennie has not finished her story.

Jennie. I did say as how I was engaged to Hicks, but I thought he would

5　　　　　59

let me off; and Mr. Yardsley looked glad when I said that, and said he'd make it all right with Hicks.

Yardsley. What? I? Jennie O'Brien, or whatever your horrible name is, do you mean to say that I said I'd make it all right with Hicks?

Jennie. Not in them words, Mr. Yardsley; but you did say as how you'd see him yourself and give him a present. You did indeed, Mr. Yardsley, as you was a-standin' on that there Proossian rug.

Dorothy. Did you, Mr. Yardsley?

[YARDSLEY *buries his face in his hands and groans.*

Barlow. Not so ready with your explanations now, eh?

Dorothy. Mr. Barlow, really I must ask you not to interfere. Did you say that, Mr. Yardsley?

Yardsley. I did, but—

Dorothy (frigidly). Go on, Jennie.

Jennie. Just then the front-door bell rings and Mr. Barlow comes, and there wasn't no more importunity for me to speak; but when I got down-stairs into the kitchen, mum, Mr. Hicks he comes in, an' *(sobs)*—an' I breaks with him.

Yardsley. You've broken with Hicks for me?

Jennie. Yes, I have—but I wouldn't never have done it if I'd known—boo-hoo—as how you'd behave this way an' deny ever havin' said a word. I—I—I l-lo-love Mr. Hicks, an' I—I hate you—and I wish I'd let him come up and kill you, as he said he would.

Dorothy. Jennie! Jennie! be calm! Where is Hicks now?

Yardsley. That's so. Where is Hicks? I want to see him.

Jennie. Never fear for that. You'll see him. He's layin' for you outside. An' that, Miss Dorothy, is why I was a-wavin' at him an' sayin' "pst" to him. I wanted to warn him, mum, of his danger, mum, because Hicks is very vi'lent, and he told me in so many words as how he was a-goin' to *do—him—up*.

Barlow. You'd better inform Mr. Hicks, Jennie, that Mr. Yardsley is already done up.

Yardsley. Do me up, eh? Well, I like that. I'm not afraid of any coachman in creation as long as he's off the box. I'll go see him at once.

Dorothy. No — no — no. Don't, Mr. Yardsley; don't, I beg of you. I don't want to have any scene between you.

Yardsley (heroically). What if he succeeds? I don't care. As Barlow says, I'm done up as it is. I don't want

A Proposal Under Difficulties

to live after this. What's the use.
Everything's lost.

Barlow (*dryly*). Jennie hasn't thrown
you over yet.

Jennie (*sniffing airily*). Yes, she has,
too. I wouldn't marry him now for all
the world — an' — an' I've lost — lost
Hicks. (*Weeps.*) Him as was so brave,
an' looks so fine in livery!

Yardsley. If you'd only give me a
chance to say something—

Barlow. Appears to me you've said
too much already.

Dorothy (*coldly*). I — I don't agree
with Mr. Barlow. You—you haven't
said enough, Mr. Yardsley. If you have
any explanation to make, I'll listen.

Yardsley (*looks up gratefully. Suddenly his face brightens. Aside*). Gad!
The very thing! I'll tell the exact
truth, and if Dorothy has half the

63

sense I think she has, I'll get in my proposal right under Barlow's very nose. (*Aloud.*) My — my explanation, Miss Andrews, is very simple. I — ah — I cannot deny having spoken every word that Jennie has charged to my account. I did get down on my knees on the rug. I did say "divine creature." I did not put it strong enough. I should have said "divinest of *all* creatures."

Dorothy (*in remonstrance*). Mr. Yardsley!

Barlow (*aside*). Magnificent bluff! But why? (*Rubs his forehead in a puzzled way.*) What the deuce is he driving at?

Yardsley. Kindly let me finish. I did say "I love you." I should have said "I adore you; I worship you." I did say, "Will you be my wife?" and I was going to add, "for if you will not,

64

then is light turned into darkness for me, and life, which your 'yes' will render radiantly beautiful, will become dull, colorless, and not worth the living." That is what I was going to say, Miss Andrews—Miss Dorothy—when—when Jennie interrupted me and spoke the word I most wish to hear—spoke the word "yes"; but it was not her yes that I wished. My words of love were not for her.

Barlow (*perceiving his drift*). Ho! Absurd! Nonsense! Most unreasonable! You were calling the sofa the divinest of all creatures, I suppose, or perhaps asking the—the piano to put on its shoes and—elope with you. Preposterous!

Dorothy (*softly*). Go on, Mr. Yardsley.

Yardsley. I—I spoke a little while

65

ago about sand — courage — when it comes to one's asking the woman he loves the greatest of all questions. I was boastful. I pretended that I had that courage; but—well, I am not as brave as I seem. I had come, Miss Dorothy, to say to you the words that fell on Jennie's ears, and—and I began to get nervous—stage-fright, I suppose it was—and I was foolish enough to rehearse what I had to say—to you, and to you alone.

Barlow. Let me speak, Miss Andrews. I—

Yardsley. You haven't anything to do with the subject in hand, my dear Barlow, not a thing.

Dorothy. Jennie—what—what have you to say?

Jennie. Me? Oh, mum, I hardly knows what to say! This is suddenter

66

than the other; but, Miss Dorothy, I'd
believe him, I would, because—I—I
think he's tellin' the truth, after all, for
the reason that—oh dear—for—

Dorothy. Don't be frightened, Jennie.
For what reason?

Jennie. Well, mum, for the reason
that when I said "yes," mum, he didn't
act like all the other gentlemen I've
said yes to, and — and k - kuk - kiss
me.

Yardsley. That's it! that's it! Do
you suppose that if I'd been after
Jennie's yes, and got it, I'd have let a
door-bell and a sofa stand between me
and—the sealing of the proposal?

Barlow (aside). Oh, what nonsense
this all is! I've got to get ahead of this
fellow in some way. (*Aloud.*) Well,
where do I come in? I came here, Miss
Andrews, to tell you—

A Proposal Under Difficulties

Yardsley (interposing). You come in where you came in before—just a little late—after the proposal, as it were.

Dorothy (her face clearing and wreathing with smiles). What a comedy of errors it has all been! I—I believe you, Mr. Yardsley.

Yardsley. Thank Heaven! And—ah —you aren't going to say anything more, D—Dorothy?

Dorothy. I'm afraid—

Yardsley. Are you going to make me go through that proposal all over again, now that I've got myself into so much trouble saying it the first time—Dorothy?

Dorothy. No, no. You needn't— you needn't speak of it again.

Barlow (aside). Good! That's *his* congé.

Yardsley. And — then if I — if I

needn't say it again? What then?
Can't I have—my answer now? Oh,
Miss Andrews—

Dorothy (*with downcast eyes, softly*).
What did Jennie say?

Yardsley (*in ecstasy*). Do you mean it?

Barlow. I fancy—I fancy I'd better
go now, Miss—er—Miss Andrews. I—
I—have an appointment with Mr.
Wilkins, and—er—I observe that it is
getting rather late.

Yardsley. Don't go yet, Jack. I'm
not so anxious to be rid of you now.

Barlow. I must go—really.

Yardsley. But I want you to make
me one promise before you go.

Dorothy. He'll make it, I'm sure, if
I ask him. Mr. Yardsley and I want
you—want you to be our best man.

Yardsley. That's it, precisely. Eh,
Jack?

Barlow. Well, yes. I'll be—second-best man. The events of the afternoon have shown my capacity for that.

Yardsley. Ah!

Barlow. And I'll show my sincerity by wearing Bob's hat and coat into the street now and letting the fury of Hicks fall upon me.

HICKS

Jennie. If you please, Miss Dorothy—I—I think I can attend to Mr. Hicks.

Dorothy. Very well. I think that would be better. You may go, Jennie.

[JENNIE *departs.*

Barlow. Well, good-day. I—I've had a very pleasant afternoon, Miss—

Andrews. Thanks for the—the cambric tea.

70

A Proposal Under Difficulties

Dorothy. Good-bye, and don't forget.

Barlow. I'm afraid—I won't. Good-bye, Bob. I congratulate you from my heart. I was in hopes that I should have the pleasure of having you for a best man at *my* wedding, but—er—there's many a slip, you know, and I wish you joy.

> [YARDSLEY *shakes him by the hand, and* BARLOW *goes out. As he disappears through the portières* YARDSLEY *follows, and, holding the curtain aside, looks after him until the front - door is heard closing. Then he turns about.* DOROTHY *looks demurely around at him, and as he starts to go to her side the curtain falls.*

THE END

Reprint Publishing

FOR PEOPLE WHO GO FOR ORIGINALS.

This book is a facsimile reprint of the original edition. The term refers to the facsimile with an original in size and design exactly matching simulation as photographic or scanned reproduction.

Facsimile editions offer us the chance to join in the library of historical, cultural and scientific history of mankind, and to rediscover.

The books of the facsimile edition may have marks, notations and other marginalia and pages with errors contained in the original volume. These traces of the past refers to the historical journey that has covered the book.

ISBN 978-3-95940-050-3

www.reprintpublishing.com